Ethereality

Ethereality

A Poetry Chapbook

By Libby L. Taylor

First paperback edition September 2020.

ISBN: 9798687677783

Book cover courtesy of Birmingham Museums Trust.

This book is dedicated to anyone who has ever
inspired me to believe in myself.

"You must stay drunk on writing so reality cannot destroy you."

- Ray Bradbury

Contents

E t h e r e a l i t y

I lay on a bed of sapphire waves

The tide gently kisses my skin

And I am embraced by its depth

I don't feel the cold of the ocean water

I am calm in the perpetual space around me

As I drift further and further into the deep

I feel

      Weightless

             Serene

   Ethereal.

"Ethereality" was originally published in Calm Down Literary Magazine's Undulating issue.

An Untitled Piece

Images of days-gone-by float around me

Like a window into the memories of my life

As I travel through the past I realise I am alone

Yet I keep dancing

To the melody

Of my memories.

The Old Man and His Memories

Pictures hanging on the wall smile at me

Their tone grey and dark

Yet when I look at them, they light up the room
with colour.

I look at myself back then; glossy hair, smooth
skin

Surrounded by the people I loved

All gone now.

I catch a glimpse of an old man in the reflection
of the pictures

He is now all I can focus on

His aged face concealing a time of youth.

See, back then all I dreamt of was the future

And before I knew it, I was old and alone

Dreaming of the past.

"The Old Man and His Memories" was originally published in Vaughan Street Doubles' third issue.

14th July

The day you left I woke up late for work and
rushed

To get the tram from Birley to town

I made it onto the platform and as I sat

I saw an old couple hand-in-hand and I smiled

Thinking of you and nana, and that I would call
later on

I still had time, right?

But as it turned out I got the call first

And my life changed as I knew it

Suddenly everyone was there, where you
wanted them to be

Ironic that the thing you wanted most

Only came when it was too late

I thought I had time.

"14th July" was originally published by Flare Literary Journal.

A Ghost and Me

This is the story of a ghost and me

I see him when I catch a glimpse of movement in the corner of my eye

And in the reflection of the old oak cabinet

I feel the brush of him walking past me in the hallway in the middle of the night

I am not afraid.

The ghost is like a distant comfort; a brief reminder that he has found his way back

The man that held me as a new-born child and witnessed my very first steps

Someone who expanded my imagination with tales of a life

Generations before my own

I am not afraid.

I watch him now as he steps into the faded light of the room

He looks different from the last time that I saw him; back straighter, cheeks fuller

He sits down beside me and tells me he is alright now

The aching feeling of his absence no longer compresses in my chest as we sit together

I am not afraid.

H o m e

In the outskirts of Leicestershire there is a place
I like to go

A village only few know

A place I call home

As I walk along the cobbled streets

Memories drift around me like wind blowing
through the trees

Once it seemed like the biggest place on earth

Now it feels so very small

I think of myself so young running on the path I
am taking now

I can almost hear the echo of my laughs fading
in the breeze

And I smile at the memories of my youth

As my heart tugs on the thought of how much I
have changed through the years

But my little village hasn't changed at all.

Longing to Belong

Where are you from?

Now and then I like to think I am from the place
of vast expanses of green

The place with the clean wind that blows
through the hidden meadows

Filled with the soft daisy flowers I would make
chains out of

Along the glittering stream that flows along the
brook outside of my old house

As I walk through the streets I feel like this is
where I should be

But the nagging thought in the back of my mind
pulls me from my reverie

And makes me feel foreign in the place I was
born.

Where are you from?

There is another place I like to think I can call
my own

A place made grey by the industrial city

With snippets of green from the hills that look down at me

Blinking lights shine like stars, letting me know that I'm not alone

I didn't grow here as a child, but I grew here into *someone*

But as I walk through the crowds of people in the streets

I wonder if I could ever claim this as my own.

Where are you from?

Whether I am here or whether I am there

I know that a part of me will always belong to each place

A younger, more innocent version of myself belongs in the overgrown meadows

And a newer version, ready to make a new start belongs in the busy city

As I make my way to new places that I can call home

I know that I have the memories of the past waiting for me

In the places I am from.

Meadow Road

There is a house that stands in the middle of a quiet street

A semi-detached red brick house with a small front garden

And a long driveway with a path of pebbles beside it

Leading to a garage with a big red door

I stand in front of it under the baking heat of the sun

Once I called this place my home

Now it feels familiar, yet so foreign.

Once upon a time this house felt so much love and laughter

But as I look at it now it is just a reminder of what came after

I dream of going back to be a child

Running up the driveway and into the comfort of the house

Everything is okay

But I know that is impossible, this isn't my home anymore

I say goodbye to the childhood that could have been

And the part of me that will always remain here

As I start a path towards a better future.

"Meadow Road" was originally published by Eris & Eros Review.

South Common

The field was ablaze with the radiant shades of
green lit up by the light of the morning sky

The rich heat of the sun beat down on the back
of my neck

As my senses awoke to the wonderous sights
around me

The breeze in the air eased the prickle of heat
that trailed down my spine

As I took a deep breath of crisp air into my
lungs

A cluster of blackbirds chased each other along
the pull of the wind above me

And a string of horses galloped up the hill
looking out onto the old city below

The delicate yellow of the buttercups
shimmered against the ground of their bed

My eyes fell upon the sight of a blossoming
Hawthorn tree standing in the field's centre

Next to it a decaying tree dried in the harsh heat

A beaten path lead through the middle of them

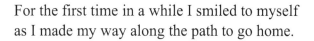

For the first time in a while I smiled to myself as I made my way along the path to go home.

"South Common" was originally published by Flare Literary Journal.

White Sheets

White sheets and cotton layers

We lay as night turns light

And day turns dark

We talk for hours

Intertwined in body and mind

My heart skips a beat whenever I look into your eyes

I can never get close enough.

Sundays In Endcliffe Park

Sun rays break through the cracks of grey-edged clouds

Trees dance to the melody of the breeze

The sound of waterfalls echoes throughout the woods

Ducks waddle along the stepping-stones in the river.

The buzz of the city is silenced by the hum of nature;

The rustle of leaves floating along the pathways

The chirping of birds in the sky

The flutter of the wings of tiny insects hovering above the flowers.

I find it difficult to leave this place

But for now, I can enjoy this moment.

Rosie, My Dog

Pepper and salt scruffy fur

With big black ears

White eyebrows fringing wide brown eyes

This is my dog, Rosie.

My true friend since the age of nine

She fills my days with laughter

Playfully bouncing along on our walks

Her face always so happy.

She knows each member of the family's names

And waits patiently when she knows they are coming

She watches the world go on through the front window

Standing on her hind legs to get a better view.

Imagining a life without my dog in it is impossible

The sweetest and funniest pet I have ever known

A pretty little schnauzer sits and smiles at me

This is my dog, Rosie.

Tiba, My Cat

A small cat lays in the garden

Fast asleep on her back, her paws in the air

She is quite the unique cat;

A glossy coat of brown and black

A fluffy mane of white on her chest

With a ginger patch around her left eye.

Her eyes snap open to the flutter of wings

A small robin rests on the fence

She studies it for a moment, ready to make a
pounce

The little bird oblivious she shifts just a bit

Then slumps back into the grass.

"Not just now" she thinks

And goes back to sleep.

The Fight

I stand on a mountain built by the generations
before me

Carved from their struggles

Wondering what I can do

To leave my legacy.

Pseudo Trends

Those who have lived on the better side of the
class divide

Are quick to use the lives of the poor as a
costume

Though they have the comfort of a bed to
themselves each night

And the ability to rest without the worry of the
nip of the cold

When they don't have the money to top up their
electric key.

They can enjoy risqué trends at leisure and
without the concern for consequences

Whilst their peers criminalise those deemed not
good enough for the same actions

The culture of the working class is taken by the
privileged

Who fail to hide their hatred for those they
fetishize.

The standards of today's society are reflected in the lives of the oppressed

As their struggles are overlooked and forged by the wealthy into masks

That they can so easily take off.

The Forgotten Ones

Our homes are made from backstreet alleys and
bus stops

As we sit, begging for charity

But you don't like us

                      You don't trust us

We don't have the money for new clothes

Yet you say we pollute the streets with our
unclean smell

                      We were once like you

We had houses, jobs, a family

But somewhere along the way it all went wrong.

Instead of being part of the crowd

We were tossed to the side-lines

                      Watching on and on.

The Faces of Change

We are powerful

We fight with a fire inside of us

Igniting us as one

A fire that has ignited

As the world wakes up

To the senseless killing of innocent lives

Their murderers walk free

Hiding behind a uniform

We will not stop

Until there is change and justice

We will be brave

We will not fall.

"The Faces of Change" was originally published by Yellow Paint Magazine as part of "Libby Taylor's Poetry on Racism" collection.

Murderers Walk Free

I can't breathe

He could hear the pedestrian's screams to get
the officer off him

Someone who swore an oath to serve and
protect

Crushed an innocent man's face harder into the
ground

As he knelt on his neck

Was it because he was black?

Or was it because a uniform allows these things
to happen

The officer told him to stop resisting but he
couldn't move

Where is the justice when life after life is taken?

And murderers are allowed to walk free

Where is the justice?

He was human too.

"Murderers Walk Free" was originally published by Yellow Paint Magazine as part of "Libby Taylor's Poetry on Racism" collection.

The World In Crisis

When all of this is over

May we take a step back

To remember the time when the world stopped

When Mother Nature began to take her own
back;

And the pollution in the rivers disappeared

And the fish returned

The birds soared through clear skies

And we took the title of most selfish species

Turning our backs on our own;

The elderly left without bread

Mothers left without milk for their children

Doctors and nurses, who we go to for help

Left without enough food to make a meal.

When all of this is over

We shall look back on this time

And realise how cruel we really were.

"The World in Crisis" was originally published by Pendemic Literary Magazine and archived in the University College Library, Dublin, as part of the Special Collections unit to remember the Covid-19 crisis for the next 50-100 years.

After

When we return to normality
I would like to think that;
We shall hug our family a little tighter
Stay with our friends a little longer
And when we see strangers in the street
I hope we can be that little bit kinder.

I hope we can all take away from this time
To not take the little things for granted;
Breathe in the crisp air on the hilltops
Savour that bagel from your local bakery
Go explore the nature on your doorstep.

I hope we can all simply enjoy life that little bit
more.

"After" was originally published by Pendemic Literary Magazine and archived in the University College Library, Dublin, as part of the Special Collections unit to remember the Covid-19 crisis for the next 50-100 years.

Mountain Climber

She is so familiar to the crumbling feeling of
defeat

The disappointing sensation erupting through
her body

As another obstacle rises in front of her,
awaiting her climb.

She doesn't realise that she has just defeated a
mountain of challenge

As she has done so many times throughout her
life,

Pushing herself to go higher

As she has risen from nothing.

So, who can blame her

When she can't see the beautiful sights of
success around her

When she is so focused on the next height in
front of her.

Solitude

I find the beauty in loneliness

Like a tigress in the Amazon

At one with my thoughts

At one with my pain

I learn to cope with my misfortunes

By just living

As what is life without pain

And a tigress without loneliness.

My Craft

My canvas is a sheet of paper

A place where the words I am unable to speak

Are unwrapped to fill each corner with colour

Spilling out the stories of my creative thought

Letting a library of artistry speak for me.

New Beginnings

It was in that moment I realised I didn't need to find myself in others

What is truly *me* is this mind I am lucky to have

Full of;

> Wonder

> Mystery

> Passion

Sheltered by the shield of my body

> Each curve telling a story

> Each imperfection perfect

As I run my fingers over my skin

I know that,

I don't need to give myself to the predation of others

Desperately trying to pull the sanctuary apart;

The sanctuary of my spirit

Because where I am most content

Is in my body, mind, and spirit

Holding onto myself.

"New Beginnings" was read by Libby at the Lincoln Festival of Creativity Poetry Reading in April 2019.

A Note From The Author

The process of writing *Ethereality* hasn't been a short one. The idea of even publishing a book of poetry hadn't occurred to me when most of these poems had been written – I had been unknowingly writing this book for over a year and a half.

Throughout the second semester of my first year at university in early 2019, I would write multiple poems a week to share with my seminar group and my tutor. Beforehand I had zero confidence in most of my writing, especially poetry. I just didn't think it would be good enough. However, over this period of time my confidence grew. From receiving really nice feedback in my class I decided to write more poetry just for myself rather than to just take into my seminars.

In April 2019 I went to a poetry reading at the *Lincoln Festival of Creativity* where I read *New Beginnings* to a small group of people. It was at this point I knew I wanted to do more with my poetry, and I decided to create an Instagram page and blog to share my work online.

Luckily I received a lot of love for my poems and my social pages grew. This increased my desire to write more and improved my confidence in being a writer.

It wasn't until March 2020 I finally decided to take what was for me, a major step, and submit my work to a literary journal in the hopes of being published. I sent *The Old Man and His Memories,* a poem I wrote a year prior, to *Vaughan Street Doubles*. A month later it was published. I was so ecstatic that a piece of mine was loved by someone else other than me – enough so to be published in an international literary journal.

From here on I would continue to send my poems to literary journals and magazines, receiving rejections, but more and more acceptations.

Other poems that I wrote were published in *Eris & Eros Review* and *Flare Literary Journal.* I had a small poetry collection tackling racism published by *Yellow Paint Magazine,* and two of my poems about the Covid-19 pandemic were published by *Pendemic Literary Magazine.* These two poems will also be archived in the University College Library, Dublin, for the next 50-100 years as part of social history. As well as poetry, I also had a short story published by *Analogies & Allegories Literary Magazine* and a film review essay published by *Ice Lolly Review*. On the side I also began to write nonfiction articles. I became a news journalist for my university's newspaper where my articles were published. I also began to write my own smaller articles on my blog. My writing experience was growing and growing.

All of these accomplishments were amazing, and I was over-the-moon with what I had achieved. For someone who had zero confidence in writing poetry, to have multiple published a year later was a big deal for me.

Throughout my life I have always known that I want to write and publish a book. However, before university especially, my main goal was to publish a novella. I didn't really know how I could go about writing a poetry book and wasn't even sure if I had enough work to even publish one. It was at this point I discovered chapbooks. I spent a little while researching them and I decided I wanted to turn my poetry into one.

I wanted to group poems that could represent life in all of its beautiful ways, and all of the ways it can throw hurdles at us, and just be, well, not-so-beautiful. I knew from the get-go that I didn't want just one simple theme of my book, I wanted to explore everything.

I compiled the poems I thought could represent the messiness of life, whether the poems had been previously published, or they had been hiding away in my drawer. These poems explored life from its beautiful moments, such as walks in the park, pets and love, to dealing with grief, loneliness, trying to discover who you are. Other poems explored living during a pandemic and a civil rights movement.

My book shows life in all of its messy ways, and I couldn't thank you enough for reading it.

The journey of making this book has been almost two years in the making, from being too shy to read my poems out in class, to getting my first poem published, to now, my first poetry chapbook is published.

Of course, this book is dedicated to all of my loved ones who have supported me along the way, but it is also dedicated to all of the readers who have given me the confidence to carry on writing.

Thank you for reading my book.

About The Author

Libby L. Taylor is a British, globally published poet and writer. Her work has featured in a range of literary journals such as, *Vaughan Street Doubles, Yellow Paint Magazine, Pendemic, Eris & Eros review* and *Flare Literary Journal.*

Her debut poetry chapbook, *Ethereality*, explores the beautiful, and not-so-beautiful parts of life.

She is currently an undergraduate student in English Literature and Creative Writing where she continues to write both poetry and short stories.

When she is not writing, you can usually find her with her nose in some kind of fantasy novel.

To find out more, visit Libby's social media pages:

Author Website: libbyltaylor.wixsite.com

Facebook page: libbyltaylor

Instagram: libbyltaylor

Twitter: libbytaylorr

Ethereality

Noun The quality or condition of being ethereal;
incorporeity; spiritually.

From The Century Dictionary.

Printed in Great Britain
by Amazon